MIRROR
MIRROR

MIRROR MIRROR

Edgar J. Hyde

CCP

© 1998 Children's Choice Publications

Text supplied by Joan Love

ISBN 1-90201-210-0

Printed and bound in the UK

Contents

Chapter 1

Sophie stood, transfixed. The doll wearing the silver, sparkling dress twirled gracefully on her stand. The tune to which the little ballerina performed her movements was now so faint that Sophie had to incline her head towards the music box. To all other onlookers, the doll was worth only a quick glance - some perhaps smiling as they remembered having such a toy when they themselves were children. The dainty satin slippers were discoloured, and most of the small silver sequins had fallen from the doll's dress. As she twirled around and came back to face Sophie, the child noticed that only part of the doll's upper lip had retained the red stain put there many years before.

"I can fix you, though," thought Sophie. "I can make you good as new."

To her, the doll was utterly magical, and she decided there and then that she had to have it. She would not leave the shop today unless she carried the ballerina with her.

From the corner of her eye, she looked at her mother and father. They were both deep in conversation with the owner of the shop - an elderly man whom Sophie had known since she had come to the shop as a tiny little girl, brought here by her parents and two older sisters. Her eldest sister, Amy-Beth was perched atop a pile of orange crates in the corner, pensively staring out of the window, the antiques shop holding no interest for her. Sophie shuddered. There could be spiders inside those crates, spiders as big as your arm – not that they would scare Amy-Beth – she really should have been a boy! Dressed in old jeans and an ill-fitting jumper, Amy-Beth was

Chapter 1

indeed the original tomboy. Her beautiful long
blond hair was scraped back from her face and
held in place with a red ribbon – one of the
few concessions she was prepared to make to
the fact that she was female. Her eyes left
Amy-Beth and travelled to where Lucy sat,
head bowed, as always, devouring every
word of every book she could lay her hands
on. Sophie herself had never understood this
attraction to words which her middle sister
felt. Though she read adequately enough for
a seven-year-old, it was a skill she used spar-
ingly, preferring instead to stare at the glossy
magazines her mother sometimes bought, or
the ones scattered around in the local hair-
dressing salon.

She suddenly became aware that her (for
she already thought of it as hers) ballerina was
still. The music had stopped and Sophie bent
forward to pick up the box and re-start the
music.

Mr and Mrs Johnson were, for once, in
complete agreement. They had been struck on

entering the shop by the beautiful gilt-edged mirror which hung above the long shop counter. Mrs Johnson was in fact so taken aback by the mirror's beauty she had gasped aloud. Her husband had been a little more non-committal until he had checked the price tag but, finding it was within their range, agreed with his wife that it would indeed look very agreeable hung above the fireplace of their newly decorated study.

"Come on girls," said Mr Johnson, "it's time to leave."

Amy-Beth and Lucy joined their parents as they said their farewells to old Mr Lawson.

"I'll have it delivered the day after tomorrow," he was saying. "Give you time to decide exactly where you're going to hang it," he laughed.

Mrs Johnson turned and walked towards where Sophie still stood. "What's this now?" her mother smiled gently. Wasn't it just typical of Sophie to find the prettiest thing in the shop.

Chapter 1

"Oh Mum," Sophie looked up into her mother's eyes, "I promise I'll do without pocket money forever if I can just have this ballerina today."

Mrs Johnson hid her smile as she lifted the little music box to check for a price. 'Forever', indeed! What rash promises these children made - promise you the Kingdom of Heaven and all for a £2.50 music box. For indeed, that was the price scrawled in large blue letters on the card attached to the foot of the ballerina. She looked at her husband. He smiled and shrugged his shoulders before ruffling Sophie's hair.

"Go on then, love, but I think maybe two weeks without pocket money would be long enough."

"Oh Dad, Mum, thanks, you've made me the happiest girl in the whole world, and I'll take such good care of her, I promise."

Sophie was breathless with the excitement of it all, and almost ran to the counter to watch Mr Lawson wrap her treasure.

"Well now, ain't that a coincidence right enough," said Mr Lawson as he picked up the little box. "Came from the same house as the mirror your Mum and Dad have just bought. Good taste you've got in this family eh?"

Mr Lawson had previously been telling Mr and Mrs Johnson how the mirror had been owned by a Lord of the Manor somewhere in Weybridge and, before that, it had been owned by previous Lords, royalty even, and passed down through the centuries.

The Johnsons listened to what the old man had to say, and looked interested enough in the history of the mirror. They had heard his stories before, stories that they felt were embroidered with just enough romance and danger as to entice the potential customers into parting with their money.

Not that they doubted there wasn't at least an element of truth in what Mr Lawson said – it was just that he tended to stretch the truth a little at times.

"Seen a lot, that mirror," he'd said earlier, and now he said the same of the little ballerina. "I wonder what stories she'd tell if only she could speak," he winked at Sophie as he finished wrapping the box in tissue paper.

Sophie smiled back. She'd read somewhere that it was very unladylike for a girl to wink, and so decided that a smile would be more fitting. She took the parcel from the old man and thanked him graciously before joining her sisters at the door of the shop.

"Should have been born a lady, that one," smiled Mr Lawson.

Mrs Johnson smiled back as she surveyed her three daughters. "How", she asked herself for the millionth time, "was it possible to have three children so utterly different from one another?"

Amy-Beth was thirteen years old and in her first year at High School; blessed with good looks, long blond hair in perfect condition, despite doing nothing with it except to tie it back from her face. The worst tragedy in her whole life was the fact that she had to wear a skirt to school.

"Should definitely have been a boy, my first born, not a female hormone in her body!"

She looked now towards Lucy. Mrs Johnson knew every curl on top of her twelve-year-old daughter's head, since that was the part of her she saw most often. Lucy spent every waking hour (and some when she should have been sleeping) with her head bowed over whatever book she was currently reading. Ever since her primary teachers had led her into the land of the printed word, Lucy had shown such an incredible thirst for knowledge, her parents hadn't known quite how to satisfy her. If she went outside to play with the local children, she could be seen perched alone on a step reading a book – sometimes even ones intended for someone several years her junior, simply because it was the only one available to her at the time. For some reason, she could not stop herself from picking up any book and losing herself in the words contained inside. Of course, her school teachers were delighted, and even more so when Lucy began to show the same love of words as she expressed herself in compositions, usually coming top in class exams. She had now joined the local library, and was allowed to take home six books at a time. Of course, most people tended to return their six books within the stipulated time period, with at least two or three unread - not so with Lucy. She was back at the Library usually that same week, with every word of every book read, digested and stored away for future use.

And Sophie – pretty, angelic little Sophie – well, maybe not so angelic sometimes. Mrs Johnson counted the necklaces around her seven-year-old daughter's neck; there were four in all. She had three bracelets on her right arm, and she wore long ruby earrings – clip-ons she might add – for, although Sophie had pleaded and pleaded with both her parents, Mrs Johnson had remained firm and said "no" to pierced ears until her daughter was at least ten years old.

Mrs Johnson knew from the sheen of Sophie's fingernails that Sophie had painted them with the clear bottle that Mrs Johnson kept in her top drawer at home. Her lips, too, looked pinker than normal, and she couldn't quite tell if it was the naturally dark colour of her eyelashes that made them look so long today, or if the little girl had helped herself to her mascara. She decided to look into *that* little matter when they got home, for she was afraid Sophie would one day poke her eyes out in her endless quest for beauty. She wore a red sticky-out dress, no doubt to match the ruby earrings, white lacy tights, and red shiny shoes to finish. Pretty as a picture, and didn't she know it.

The Johnson family left the antique shop, having said their final goodbyes to Mr Lawson, amid promises of a Tuesday delivery.

"I'm glad we popped in there this morning," Mr Johnson said to his wife as he started up the car. "Now, let's go home and have lunch."

As the car climbed the hill on the last leg of the journey home, "Oatlands" came into view. Amy-Beth found the house absolutely breathtaking. It wasn't that she didn't appreciate beauty, like Sophie thought, just that she wasn't vain and looked for beauty outside of herself. The house had been built over 200 years ago and, though imposing, Amy-Beth thought it always looked friendly and welcoming as you approached. It was autumn now, the large surrounding gardens were a mass of reds, golds and oranges, helping to add to the attractive look of the house.

As yet, the Johnson family did not use all the rooms of "Oatlands", having only moved into the house some three months prior. Mrs Johnson was in no rush with the decor. "Better to wait and buy exactly what you want, rather than rushing and getting it all wrong," she was fond of saying.

Amy-Beth loved to explore and, though she had spent most of her spare time since they moved here doing just that, she still felt sure there were parts of the house she hadn't been in. As the car pulled into the driveway, she was already undoing her seat belt in preparation for her dash from the car to the basement. She had just been about to start her exploration of that area after breakfast that morning when she was called to go to the antique shop. If she hurried, she could spend at least an hour down there before Mum called her for lunch.

Mr Johnson had barely stopped the car when Amy-Beth opened the door and got out. Lucy, too, had undone her seat belt, and was getting ready to make a quick exit.

"And just where do you think you're going?" Mrs Johnson directed towards Lucy, since she had been too late in putting the same question to Amy-Beth, who was by now out of earshot.

Lucy paused, one leg already half way out

of the car door. "I've just got to finish the chapter I was reading this morning, Mum, and then I'll find out what happened to Julie-Anne. I was at a really crucial point this morning when you called me, and I couldn't concentrate properly in the antique shop, please Mum, just half an hour, then I'll come and help you prepare lunch."

Lucy smiled winningly at her mother. Though maybe not as pretty as her other daughters, Lucy had a smile that could charm the birds off the trees, and it worked on Mrs Johnson every time.

"Go on, then," she sighed. "Maybe the next time you're in the library you could get some cookery books. If you're as interested in that subject as everything else, who knows, I may even get some respite from spending my life in the kitchen."

Mr Johnson got out of the car and helped Sophie unfasten her seat belt. She got out of the car very carefully, holding the brightly-wrapped package tightly in both hands.

"If you're going to your room, Sophie, lunch will be ready in about an hour, so come down when you're called."

"Okay, Mum," Sophie smiled, and stood on tiptoe and kissed her mother. "And thanks, this is the best present ever." She turned towards her father, kissed him too, and climbed the stairs to her room.

Mr Johnson hung his coat in the small cloakroom beneath the stairs and made his way into the morning room to finish reading his newspaper.

"Nothing else for it, then," thought Mrs Johnson as she donned her apron and made her way into the kitchen. She opened the kitchen cupboards. "Now then, what's on today's menu?"

Chapter 2

"Where on earth is the first aid box," asked Mrs Johnson of no-one in particular. Indeed, if anyone knew where anything was in the house, it was bound to be her, since no-one else paid the slightest bit of attention to such chores as tidying up.

Dad apparently had cut his finger on a corner of the new mirror. It had been delivered, as promised, on Tuesday morning and Dad had spent most of the morning trying to hang it on the wall above the fireplace. Eventually, after much banging, taking down, muttering, and some tutting from his wife, he had managed to get the mirror hanging in just the right spot. On his way down the ladder, however, he had ripped his thumb on a jagged part of the gilt surrounding the mirror, hence the search for the first aid box.

Mrs Johnson came out of the kitchen carrying the thought-to-be-missing box and proceeded into the study where her injured husband sat feeling very sorry for himself. She wiped his finger, and generally fussed over him, making much of the "fabulous" job he had made of hanging the mirror. A few minutes later, a bandaged Mr Johnson was smiling again. His wife knew that his ego only needed flattering, and a bit of a fuss made over him, before he would be back to his normal self. He practically strutted round the room, turning from every corner to see what the mirror looked like from that angle.

"Yes, it does look rather good, dear, even if I do say so myself," he said, for all the world sounding as if he had made the whole mirror, rather than just hanging it from a nail in the wall. Mrs Johnson, however, knew when to keep quiet, and merely mumbled her agreement.

"Once we're actually using the room, perhaps we can buy wall lights. If we put them at a certain angle, it would show the mirror off to its best advantage," said Mr Johnson.

"Yes dear," agreed his wife, as she ushered him out of the room. "But that's after we have the chimney swept, the gas connected, and have paid a visit to the gas showroom to pick a suitable fire. I'm afraid there's a lot to be done to that room yet before we can start using it properly."

The three girls, too, had admired the mirror. It really was quite imposing hanging there, though little Sophie was too small to see herself unless she stood on tiptoe.

"Come on, you two," said Amy-Beth, the explorer, "there is much to see and do and so little time to do it all."

Lucy, book tucked under her arm, followed her older sister from the room. Not that she was going to do any exploring – at least nothing outside chapter nine of her book!

Sophie, then, was alone in the room. She soon worked out that if she sat on the top of her father's leather-covered desk, she could see herself in the mirror.

Today, she was wearing "Crimson Tide" nail enamel. Mum had said she could wear bright colours when she wasn't in school, and she had spent the best part of the morning applying the bright colour to her tiny, but perfectly shaped, fingernails. At breakfast earlier that day, she had admired them from every angle, holding her cereal spoon in such a way as to show them to their best advantage. Though if she'd hoped her sisters would show any interest in her nails, she was soon proved wrong. Amy-Beth spent the whole of the morning meal quizzing her father about the history of the house. And Lucy? Well Lucy was, quite unbelievably, reading the back of the cornflakes packet. Sophie had shaken her head and, picking up the music box that accompanied her everywhere, excused herself from the breakfast table and made her way to the study.

She hoisted herself, with some difficulty, on top of the desk, and took the matching "Crimson Tide" lipstick from her skirt pocket. She opened her lipstick case and, using the small vanity mirror, carefully applied the red colour to her lips. She smiled at herself in the large gilt mirror. "Beautiful", she thought to herself, though an onlooker would have been forgiven for thinking she looked somewhat ghoulish, with her small white face, framed by chestnut curls, finished off with too-red lip gloss. To Sophie herself, however, she was beautiful, and she didn't care to ask anyone else's opinion.

Suitably made up now, she smiled at herself, quite pleased with her reflection in the mirror. She picked up a glossy magazine and started to read from the "Helpful Hair Hints" page. She carefully positioned her fingers so that she could see the tiny little red shells glint back at her from the mirror. She decided to read aloud. She had watched, fascinated, as her Sunday School teacher read to the class each Sunday, her long nails curled around the book, her lips adorned with a bright colour that never seemed to budge, despite frequent licking of her lips. The reading aloud didn't last long, though, and before long she reached for her little music box, the ballerina now restored to her former glory. Sophie had painted the little doll's lips with one of her nail polishes, and painted the tiny little fingertips the same colour for good measure.

She wound up the box and placed it beside her on the desk and, as the music began to play, she returned to reading the "Colouring Tips." She was just wondering if her mother would have a fit if Sophie were to dye some of her curls purple when she thought she felt someone watching her. She looked up, thinking she would see only her own reflection, and was horrified to see not her own face but that of an older girl, one who looked remarkably like Lucy. Or maybe it wasn't that she looked so much like Lucy, maybe it was the fact that she had a book on her knee, opened. She wasn't looking at the book, however, she was staring straight at Sophie. Sophie sat very still and blinked hard, then turned her head quickly to look behind her. There was no-one else in the room. Certainly no-one else who could be creating this reflection that she now saw beside her. The ballerina pirouetted and turned gracefully to the music, somehow lending an air of complete unreality to the whole scene.

Sophie made to get off the desk and go and get her parents, or her sisters, but before she could do so the girl in the mirror turned her eyes away from Sophie to look at another scene which was unfolding. Terrified though she was, Sophie could not take her eyes away from the mirror, neither could she get off the desk. Her eyes followed the girl's, and the scene before her completely changed.

There were thousands upon thousands of

people, all jostling and pushing for a place in the crowd. Sophie saw a large wooden construction, some sort of scaffolding, which was draped entirely in black cloth, and strewn with straw. A lady approached the scaffolding, a young and beautiful lady, accompanied by four attendants. She wore a dark grey dress trimmed with fur, and a long white cape. In her hands, the woman clutched a prayer book, and as she approached the scaffolding she turned and gave the book to one of her attendants. The four women were weeping, and Sophie could sense the fear in the atmosphere. The crowd were becoming agitated now, jeering and shouting, fists punching the air, children being lifted onto shoulders. The beautiful lady, her hair bound high, knelt at the block on the scaffolding and unclasped her necklace. A hooded man, dressed completely in black, who Sophie would later learn was the headsman, spoke briefly to the lady and knelt to retrieve his hidden axe from the straw. Just as Sophie realised what was about to happen,

Chapter 2

the headsman brought his axe first high up into the air then brought it down swiftly, cutting off the woman's head. Sophie cried out in horror. She glanced at the young girl in the mirror and thought she saw tears on her face, too. As the severed head fell into the straw in front of the block, the headsman picked it up and showed it to the cheering crowd. Sophie screamed, louder this time, and, no longer frozen to the desk, jumped down and fled the study as quickly as her young legs would allow.

"Mum, Dad, anyone, help me, help me!" she ran along the hallway, shouting loudly. She almost jumped out of her skin when she ran straight into Amy-Beth, who had just come from the kitchen.

"For Heaven's sake, Sophie, what on earth's got into you?" Amy-Beth clasped the young girl firmly by the shoulders. "Calm down," she told the shaking girl, "and tell me what this is all about."

"Oh Amy-Beth it was horrible! They murdered her, they were glad she died. There was a man with a hood, and the little girl was so sad, I think she was crying, too, and the blood was everywhere in the straw."

"Hold on, Sophie, just hold on. Were you watching a scary video, because if you were, I just might have to tell Mum, if this is the effect it's going to have on you."

"It wasn't a video, Amy-Beth, oh please don't shout at me, I didn't do anything wrong, honestly, it was the mirror! I was just looking in the mirror, and something horrible happened! I don't understand it, I don't."

By this time, Lucy too had appeared, and stopped to find out what all the to-do was about.

"Come on, Sophie, come into the kitchen and sit down. Maybe if you calm down a little, you can tell us exactly what happened."

Lucy took her little sister by the hand and led her into the comfort of the warm kitchen. The three sisters sat round the table.

"Okay, Sophie, if you're feeling any better,

start at the beginning and maybe we can figure this whole thing out," said Amy-Beth.

And so she did. She began at the beginning, from when she'd picked up her magazine, to when she wound up her music box, to when she was drawn to the scene in the mirror. The two older girls looked at one another.

"Well, if I didn't know better, I'd say you'd been reading up on some history, Henry Vlll or something," said Lucy. "It sounds just like the scene of one of his wives being beheaded."

Amy-Beth dug Lucy hard in the ribs. "Don't frighten her any more than she already is," she chided her sister. "Come on, Sophie, let's go back to the study and see what we can find."

Sophie was aghast. "But I can't go back in there! please Amy-Beth, don't make me go back into the study, it frightens me too much. Please, I'll do anything you say, only don't make me go back into that room!"

"Hush, Sophie," said Amy-Beth, placing an

arm round her young sister's shoulders. "I won't make you do anything you don't want to, don't worry. Lucy and I will go. You stay here, and we'll be right back."

Sophie wiped her eyes, forgetting for the moment the eyeshadow she had so carefully applied that morning, and which she had now smeared all over her tear-stained little face.

"Where are Mum and Dad, anyway?" she wanted to know.

"They've just gone down to the market for a while – perhaps just as well, I think. We don't really want them seeing you this upset till we know exactly what's going on."

Lucy poured her little sister a glass of milk, put two chocolate cookies on a plate and, having made sure she was all right to be left alone for a few minutes, the two girls left the kitchen and made their way towards the study.

Amy-Beth pushed open the door. The two girls were greeted by quietness, the smell of old leather, and a general air of peace. Lucy bent over and picked up her sister's music box from where it lay on the floor.

"Look, she must have dropped it when she ran from the room," she said.

Amy-Beth nodded. "She must have been really frightened to leave her ballerina anywhere, that's for sure."

Amy-Beth walked towards the mirror, looking for any clues as to what had taken place in the study only minutes before. The mirror looked like, well, a mirror! She stood on tiptoe and touched around the edges, trying to feel if there could possibly be something behind it. She turned away from the mirror, then turned back quickly to look at her reflection – nothing save her own face.

"I feel a bit daft doing this," she thought, shaking her head. She didn't want to dislodge the mirror from its place on the wall after all the trouble her father had taken getting it to hang "just right", and turned to Lucy to see if she had found anything, when she spotted something lying on the carpet just in front of where she stood. She bent closer and saw that it was a piece of straw - or rather pieces of straw – pieces stuck together with blood!

"I can't believe it – it can't be!" she told herself, picking up the straw and stuffing it quickly into the pocket of her jeans.

Lucy turned: "What did you say?"

Amy-Beth was unaware she had spoken aloud. "Nothing, nothing, Lucy, I just think we're wasting our time here, there's nothing to be found, let's get back to Sophie in the kitchen."

Amy-Beth, for the time being, didn't want her younger sister seeing what she had just found – not until she had more time to examine it at least. "Come on," she led the way out of the room, "let's go."

Amy-Beth waited till Lucy had left the room, then turned to close the door. She pushed the straw deeper into her pocket then turned to her younger sister.

"And Lucy, I don't mean to go on at you or anything, I mean, I know you're well-read and all that, but I really don't think it's a good idea to plant things in Sophie's little mind."

"I know, I'm sorry, I didn't mean to do that, it's just that, honestly, Amy-Beth, she could have been describing a scene straight from the history books. I mean, Anne Boleyn died in exactly that way. She had four ladies-in-waiting with her, her executioner held her head aloft to show the crowd what happened to those who committed treason towards the King, and her hair was bound high so that it wouldn't get in the way of the headsman's axe."

Amy-Beth shivered involuntarily. "Okay, Lucy, I hear what you're saying, but quite frankly you're making the hairs stand on the back of my neck now! Please say no more of this to Sophie. Though I don't want to doubt her, I think she must have imagined this whole thing. Maybe she lapsed into a little daydream when her music box played – who knows?"

Carrying the magazine and the little ballerina, the two girls walked back along the hallway towards the kitchen. Lucy touched Amy-Beth's arm. "I've just remembered something else."

"What is it now?" asked her sister, a little impatiently.

"Well, when Anne Boleyn was being held prisoner in the Tower, she sent away one of her attendants and requested that her seven-year-old niece take her place. You see it wasn't considered unsuitable back then for a young child to be exposed to the realities of suffering and death. Maybe the little girl in the mirror. . ."

Amy-Beth had heard enough. "Lucy, if you repeat one word of that, just one word, ever again, I'll burn every book in your room. Can't you see how frightened Sophie is, and you're going to add to it with horror stories?"

"I'm not trying to scare her, Amy-Beth, it's just that there really was a seven-year-old . . ."

Lucy's words tailed off as she saw the way Amy-Beth was looking at her. "Okay, I'm sorry, I'll never mention it again." And, taking the magazine from her sister, she pushed open the kitchen door and went to comfort her younger sister as best she knew how.

Amy-Beth pushed the piece of blood sodden straw deep into her jeans' pocket. She was letting no-one see what she had found on the floor of the study until she had looked into this whole matter further!

Chapter 3

Sophie woke the next morning to find Amy-Beth in bed beside her. She touched her sister's cheek gently.

"Amy-Beth," she said softly.

Amy-Beth groaned and tried to open her eyes. "Hi, little Sis'" she said and turned onto her side. "What time is it?"

Sophie squinted at her pink heart shaped alarm clock and replied, "7:39."

"Twenty to eight?" said Amy-Beth. "Gosh, it feels like the middle of the night!"

"I'm sorry, Amy-Beth, I didn't mean to wake you, I was curious. I mean, what are you doing in my bed?"

"Don't you remember – you were having a nightmare. I was just going into my room last night and I heard you call out. You were really quite upset – don't know how you can't remember."

Sophie pulled herself up onto one elbow. "I remember being frightened before I got to sleep, Amy-Beth, but I don't remember you coming into my room."

"Well, maybe it's just as well," smiled Amy-Beth. "No point in dwelling on these things, is there? You were probably dreaming about your experience in the study, though I really do think it was a trick of your imagination."

Sophie started to protest, but her elder sister placed her index finger on the young girl's lips. "Hush now, we have to forget all about these things. Tell you what, let's surprise Mum and Dad. Let's get up early and give them both a cooked breakfast. What do you say?"

Sophie smiled. "Okay then." She jumped out of bed and donned her dressing gown.

Chapter 3

"What shall we make – pancakes?"

The two girls made their way downstairs to the kitchen. Amy-Beth shivered. "It's cold in here" she said. "Wish the heating would hurry up and come on." The words were no sooner out of her mouth when the girls heard the familiar clanking and creaking of the ancient central heating system beginning to come to life.

"There we go" she told her younger sister, "we'll soon be warm now."

When Mr and Mrs Johnson came downstairs some time later, they were greeted by the very welcome sight of freshly made pancakes, sizzling bacon and eggs in the pan, and the delicious aroma of fresh coffee.

"Well, this is a surprise," said Mrs Johnson as she kissed the top of her youngest daughter's head and joined Amy-Beth at the cooker. "To what do we owe the honour, then?" she finished.

"Nothing, Mum," replied Amy-Beth. "Sophie and I just decided it was time to give you a break from the kitchen, especially since it's Sunday. And as we both woke early enough we decided breakfast was a good time to start."

"Well, it's much appreciated, isn't it dear?" Mrs Johnson turned to her husband.

"Mmm? What's that?" he muttered, head already stuck in the sports pages of the Sunday paper he had pulled from the letter box on his way through the hallway.

"And he wonders where Lucy gets it from! I said, it's much appreciated – the girls making breakfast for us like this." Mrs Johnson pulled the paper back from husband's face and waited for his reply.

"Oh, yes, yes, sorry girls, just wanted to know the outcome of the big fight last night. Yes, it smells just delicious, I'll have two of everything," he told his wife, as he returned to his much-loved paper.

"I take it Lucy's still asleep then, Mum," said Amy-Beth, between mouthfuls of toast.

"No, she's not asleep," returned Mrs

Johnson, "she's propped up in bed, *reading* for a change!"

Amy-Beth smiled. "Whatever would that girl do without books?"

Sophie avoided the study for the rest of that week. Not that she ever had any real cause to go in there, but she did like the room, the peaceful air, the smell of old leather that somehow reminded her of her father. She spent most of her time either in her own room or with one of her sisters in theirs. Lucy helped her to dye a favourite pair of shoes. They were so discoloured Mum was going to throw them out, but the two girls made such a good job Mum said she could keep them. And so she passed her days, still playing with her little music box, and causing her parents to smile as they watched her walk upstairs with her bright yellow shoes adorned with daisy transfers on each strap.

"Auntie Patsy's coming over on Friday night," said Mum that day.

"Oh, great," said Amy-Beth. "Is she staying over?"

"She probably will be. Dad and I are going out and we may be too late back for her to get home. There's plenty of room for her to stay here, anyway" she finished.

Aunt Patsy was Mum's sister, and the three girls loved when she came to stay. She was the type of auntie any child would have loved. She never gave rows, she gave sweets on demand, watched silly videos with the children, and generally spoilt them rotten. Every time she came to their house, she arrived carrying a large holdall, inside which the girls knew would be presents for them all. A magazine for little Sophie, usually one with a free gift of lipstick on the front, a new best-seller which aunt Patsy knew Lucy wouldn't have read yet, and last time for Amy-Beth it had been brightly coloured laces for her huge, ungainly walking boots. And so, the Auntie-Patsy-visit was looked forward to with much excitement.

"Oh Mum," breathed Sophie on the night, "you look beautiful."

"Why, thank you, darling," smiled Mrs Johnson as she took one final look in the mirror. "I'm really quite thrilled I got this dress on at all, I haven't worn it for so long I doubted I would get the zip up!"

Sophie handed her mother her red gloves from the bedside table and smiled in admiration. Her Mum was swathed from head to toe in red silk, her dark hair pulled back in a chignon. Mum and Dad were going to a dance her father's office was giving, and had decided at the last minute to stay overnight at the hotel.

"You girls will be just fine with Aunt Patsy and, in case anyone suddenly goes down with measles or the black plague, I'll be leaving the hotel 'phone number with her so that she can get in touch."

Lucy had just entered her parents' bedroom. "The black plague, Mum, you're going back a bit now, aren't you? Died out years ago."

Mrs Johnson smiled. "Stranger things, my

dear, stranger things. Now, where did I put my earrings?"

She needn't have asked. Sophie was holding them against her ears while she admired herself in the mirror.

"Mum, can't I. . ."

"Now don't start the pierced-ear pleading again, Sophie, I told you before – only when you're older. You're only seven years old. Now come and give me a kiss before I put my lipstick on, and let's not fall out about silly old earrings before I go out for the night."

"Sorry Mum," Sophie hugged and kissed her mother. Lucy, too, kissed her Mum, then all three got up to go downstairs. They had just reached the top hallway when they heard the doorbell.

"That'll be Auntie Patsy" remarked Mum, "late as usual."

Mum knew her sister's timekeeping habits of old, and had learned that if she wanted Patsy to be there for 7 o'clock she had to tell her 6 o'clock, realising that she would never, ever be anywhere on time!

Amy-Beth and her father opened the door.

"Hi" beamed aunt Patsy, an even bigger bag than usual tucked under her arm. "Let me in there quickly, it's *freezing* out here."

Amy-Beth smiled. Aunt Patsy was always *freezing*, *starving* or *dying* of something. Everything in extremes, always.

Harry Johnson followed his sister-in-law into the kitchen, where everyone tended to go when they entered the house. "Let me take your coat, Patsy. Can I get you a coffee or anything?"

"Oh, that would be lovely, Harry," she handed him her coat. "My, my, you do look handsome," she said then, turning as her sister entered the room, admired her too. "Why, you'll be the belle of the ball, the envy of everyone there I should think. Now, where's that coffee before I freeze to death?"

Amy-Beth smiled. Everything in extremes, that was Auntie Patsy, all right.

Chapter 4

Aunt Patsy had carefully placed her bag just inside the kitchen door.

"Aunt Patsy," said Lucy, "I hate to tell you this, but I think your bag just moved!"

Aunt Patsy smiled. "Goodness, gracious, you can't keep secrets for long in this house." She walked over to where her bag lay and opened it up. A smallish box was produced from inside the bag, a thick cardboard box with holes in, and from the box came the sound of snuffling, followed by a frightened yelp. The girls crowded round as Aunt Patsy removed the lid. The most beautiful, fluffy,

golden little puppy looked up at everyone
with the biggest, brownest eyes they had ever
seen. Bedlam ensued. Everyone spoke at once,
the girls clamouring for a hold of the little pup.

"Oh Aunt Patsy – she's beautiful – is it a
he or a she? – is it for us? – can we keep it? –
what's his name? – what age is it? – can it sleep
in my room?"

Aunt Patsy didn't know which child asked
which question, but she tried to answer as best
she could.

"She's for the family, a sort of housewarming present, she's eight weeks old, doesn't yet
have a name, and it's up to your mother where
she sleeps."

Jill Johnson looked aghast at her sister. She
had bought them a *dog* as a housewarming
present! She'd murder her – three children, a
house not half-decorated, and now a pup! She
tried to smile, managing a sort of lop-sided
grimace.

"Well, that is a surprise, Patsy. But since it
was *such* a surprise, we obviously don't have

a basket for her to sleep in yet do we – so you'll have to think of somewhere to put her tonight until we get to the shops tomorrow. In bed with you, perhaps?" she finished sarcastically.

Patsy merely shrugged. "Sure, she can sleep with me for tonight, except she's not *quite* house-trained yet! Might be a small problem there."

She turned to look at the children, who were completely entranced by the new addition to the family, particularly Sophie. Amy-Beth was pleased, too, she felt it was just the kind of thing Sophie needed to take her mind off her experience in the study. The little pup lay contentedly in Sophie's arms, paws stuck straight out in the air, while Lucy scratched her tummy. She almost purred with the enjoyment of it all, long ears flopped over to one side.

"Oh, she's such a sweetie, Aunt Patsy, thank you, thank you!" gushed Sophie as she cuddled the little dog so tightly Aunt Patsy was fearful that the puppy food she had given it some hours previously would soon be projected over her sister's floor!

"Sweetie! What a brilliant name," said Aunt Patsy. "Well done, Sophie, you've just christened your new puppy. Sweetie – couldn't have thought of anything better myself!"

"Sweetie!?" thought Lucy and Amy-Beth at the same time. Imagine taking her for a walk when she was fully grown! She was a golden retriever after all, and they did grow fairly large – and they were to call her Sweetie! Amy-Beth gave Lucy a look that said "say nothing" for both girls knew the naming of the puppy had delighted Sophie, and neither of them wanted to upset her.

Mrs Johnson sighed resignedly. There was nothing she could do about it now – best to make the most of it and leave the family to it for tonight.

She took her coat from the cloakroom – Harry having already put the overnight bag in the boot of the car - kissed everyone firmly on the cheeks, issued more last minute instructions and, finally, left.

"Well, girls, what are we going to do tonight, then?" asked Aunt Patsy as she ushered them all through to the sitting room.

"Amy-Beth and I had been playing Scrabble earlier, but if you'd like to join in we can scrap that game and start again. We've been playing on father's desk in the study – it's easier in there, rather than trying to play on the floor," said Lucy.

"Oh no, no, don't scrap a game just for me, pet. I think I'll stay here with Sophie and Sweetie for now, but why don't you and Amy-Beth go on and finish your game - I'll know where to find you if I need you." Aunt Patsy sipped at her coffee and popped a chocolate into her mouth. "Oh, and help yourselves to some chocolate," she said, indicating the supply she had brought with her and placed on the sideboard. Both girls took some of the chocolate, gave Sweetie a final pat and left the room to go and continue their game.

"It's not very warm in here, is it?" complained Lucy as she shivered in her chair.

"It's just because there's an empty hearth, and it makes you feel that there should be a lit fire there," replied Amy-Beth, staring hard at the letters she had in front of her.

"Come on," urged Lucy, "if you'd hurry up and play I wouldn't be thinking about the cold." Absentmindedly she played with the little music box, lifting it up and putting it back down again, rufffling the edges of the doll's little skirt. "The music box – did you bring this in with you Amy-Beth?"

"Mmm? No – why would I bring that with me," replied Amy-Beth. "Sophie must have left it here."

"But Sophie hasn't been in here for ages, you know, ever since. . ." Lucy tailed off, leaving the sentence unfinished. Ah well, doesn't matter, I suppose. Will you please hurry up?"

Amy-Beth placed three letters on the board in front of her.

Chapter 4

" 'Zoo'? Is that it – it took you all this time to make 'zoo'?" said Lucy.

Amy-Beth smiled. "Yes, but just look how many points I picked up," she said.

Lucy gasped, then picked up the pieces to double check the scoring. Amy-Beth was right. Lucy sighed, before looking at her own letters to see how she could get her own back - she was winning, anyway, but she wanted to win conclusively, and by a large margin if possible!

Amy-Beth picked up the music box and she, too, began examining the little ballerina. "Beats me how she's so attached to this," she mumbled, winding it up as she spoke. "I suppose she was quite pretty once upon a time, but that must have been a very long time ago!" She placed the little doll down on the leather desk and waited patiently for Lucy to play.

The little ballerina twirled to the music and, as she did, the girls became aware of a mist swirling from the mirror. Lucy dropped the letters she had held in her hand and turned to stare.

A young girl looked at them both from inside the mirror. Amy-Beth caught her breath and reached out to grasp Lucy's hand. As the girls stared, they became aware of other people in the mirror. They could see a woman in her kitchen with her two children beside her. There seemed to be an air of panic, the woman quickly gathering items together. She lifted a torch and some blankets and took some foodstuffs from the fridge. "Come on Carly," she took her daughter's hand, "we'll have to hurry."

The little boy, too, held his mother's hand and all three left the house. Amy-Beth and Sophie had almost to cover their ears, the sound of the air-raid siren emanating from the mirror becoming deafening as it went on and on. The small party had now reached the back garden, quickly making their way towards the air raid shelter, when the little girl stopped dead.

"Trish – Mum – I've forgotten Trish, I'll have to go back for her." The woman stopped, pushing her hair from her eyes impatiently. "Carly, we *cannot go* back to the house now, and especially not for a doll! Hurry now, let's go." She regained hold of the child's hand, and made to pull her towards the shelter. The child dug her heels in fast. "I can't Mum, I can't leave her all alone, she'll be frightened, please can we go back?." Her brother tutted. "*Frightened?* It's a doll, stupid, she can't feel anything, now hurry, do what Mum says and get inside the shelter."

Carly started to cry, her brother's harsh, though true, words unleashing her tears. She tried to bite down on her lip, and drew the back of her hand across her wet cheeks. The woman's heart melted – she had never been able to bear to see any of her children cry. "Okay", she knelt beside the little girl, "okay, Carly, dry your eyes, you and your brother go into the shelter and I'll join you as soon as I have Trish.

Go on, hurry, the two of you." She gave her children a gentle push. "Don't look so worried, Tim, I'll be back before you've even closed the door, go on."

The noise of the air raid siren was deafening as the mother made her way back to the house. Amy-Beth found that she was holding her breath, willing the woman to hurry and get back to the comparative safety of the shelter. The girls watched her enter the house and, what seemed like an eternity later, descend the back stairs clutching the doll in her hand. She was halfway across the garden when the bomb dropped. Not directly on the house, it actually fell some distance away, but it was close enough to cause damage to the roof, blowing in some windows and tearing the door straight off its hinges. The woman fell, striking her head against the garden wall. Her scream could hardly be heard, there was so much noise going on all around. The door which had been torn from its hinges fell right on top of her, the glass pane shattering as it connected with her head. Aware that something was wrong, but not knowing what, the children ran from the shelter, followed by some adults trying to hang on to the children and restrain them until the planes had gone.

Carly saw her mother first, blood spattered, eyes wide open, her body contorted beneath her from how she had fallen. "Mum!" the child screamed, followed by her brother. Both ran towards the figure, screaming and crying, throwing themselves onto the ground, trying frantically to clear the debris from her. Mrs Winters, who had followed the children outside, tried to calm them both. She could tell merely by looking that their mother was dead, and clearing debris would do no good at this stage. She lifted Carly into her arms, another neighbour taking hold of Tim, speaking calming words, leading them both back into the shelter.

"We can't leave her there," choked Tim, "we can't leave her there on her own, she'll be frightened."

Lucy and Amy-Beth watched the receding figures and looked again at the dead woman. Still clutched in her hand was the little doll.

As the picture began to fade, the girl who they had first seen in the mirror reappeared. She smiled at the sisters, and they noticed that she now had the little doll on her knee, stroking her hair. Slowly, her face faded from the mirror, almost at exactly the same time as the little ballerina stopped turning to the tune played by the music box.

Amy-Beth exhaled deeply. "Are you all right?" she turned towards Lucy.

"I think so," her younger sister replied. "I simply can't quite believe what we just saw. I mean if you hadn't been with me I'd have doubted for my own sanity. Poor Sophie, that's all I can say, no wonder she ran screaming from the room when she experienced her 'sighting'."

Amy-Beth nodded in agreement. "I don't understand what's happening here at all." She stood up and walked towards the mirror.

Her face pressed almost directly against it,

Chapter 4

she tried to see if it could possibly be rigged in some way to show the scenes they had just witnessed. She pulled it slightly away from the wall, too, trying to see behind but saw nothing except for the rather faded wallpaper it covered.

"There's nothing strange here, at all," she told Lucy. She turned to look at her sister and saw the younger girl had turned deathly pale. "Are you all right?" she asked.

"Not really," Lucy replied. "I feel rather sick, in fact – shock I suppose. Scrabble's the last thing I feel like doing, I can tell you. I think I'll go and make myself a hot drink. Come with me, Amy-Beth, please, don't stay here on your own."

"No fear of that," replied Amy-Beth. "I'm right beside you. "What do we tell Aunt Patsy, if anything?"

"I don't know, Amy-Beth, I mean it does seem rather hard to believe doesn't it? And apart from anything else, if we tell Sophie we've had a 'mirror' experience we'll terrify the life out of her again, just when she seems to be forgetting it ever happened."

"Yes, I think you're right" replied Amy-Beth. "We'll say nothing for now, but tomorrow I'm going back into the study to see if anything else happens. I wonder if there's something that triggers the sightings off, a special word or something – think, Lucy, what were we doing that Sophie could have been doing when she had her experience?"

Lucy glanced down to look at the little music box, still and silent now. She pointed to the ballerina – "Playing the music box – could that be it?"

Amy-Beth looked too. "Of course, you're right, that has to be it! And remember, the day Mum and Dad bought the box for Sophie, old Mr Lawson said it had come from the same house as the mirror. Do you think, somehow, that the mirror has retained all the awful memories of everything it has ever witnessed, and they're being recounted back to us every time the music plays?"

Lucy looked dubious. "Seems rather far-fetched, I have to admit Amy-Beth, I mean who on earth would ever believe us? And who's the little girl – some sort of 'keeper of the mirror' or something? It just doesn't make any sense." She shivered involuntarily. "I really have to get out of here, let's get back to normality and go and eat some of Aunt Patsy's chocolates."

Chapter 5

Next morning Amy-Beth woke to the sound of barking. Tiny, little barks, almost squeaks, coming from Sophie's room. She got up and pulled on her housecoat and went across the hall to her sister's room.

"Oh, you're up," she said, surprised to see Sophie up and dressed, chasing Sweetie round her room with a small furry toy.

"I've been up for hours," smiled Sophie, "Sweetie jumped onto my pillow this morning and licked me awake. She's so cute, I just love her to bits. I'm so glad Aunt Patsy came to stay and brought her with her."

Amy-Beth smiled. She was glad the puppy was taking up so much of her sister's time; she only hoped she didn't get fed up having to get up in the middle of the night to attend to the little dog. She walked towards the window and sat down in the basket chair, tucking her legs beneath her. As she sat, she noticed a little doll sitting at the top of Sophie's bed, a doll which was just a bit more than familiar. The last time she had seen that doll, she knew, it had been clutched in a dead woman's hands. A shiver went right through her body. What was going on? Inwardly shaking, but trying to remain calm, she asked Sophie where she'd gotten the doll.

"She was in my room this morning, on the chair you're sitting on, I thought you or Lucy had left her for me. Didn't you?" Sophie tailed off.

Amy-Beth knew that the doll was definitely the one from the mirror, she just didn't want to believe it. The doll belonging to the little girl whose mother had been killed was in her little sister's room – who had put it there?. The whole thing was impossible. She must try and stay calm, compose herself as best she could.

"No, I didn't put it there, but it may have been Lucy, who knows. Doesn't matter anyway, does it? She's very pretty, what will you call her?"

Sophie shrugged. She didn't seem to be overly interested in the doll, instead carefully watching Sweetie as she tried to eat the contents of her doll's house.

"Funny how they try to eat everything isn't it?"

Amy-Beth agreed as she got up to leave. She picked up the doll, without Sophie noticing and left the room to go and see Lucy. "Breakfast will be soon, Sophie, come downstairs when you're ready."

Almost running along the hallway, Amy-Beth burst into Lucy's room. Lucy was still asleep, but not for long.

"Lucy, Lucy, come on, you have to wake

up, you're not going to believe what I have to show you."

Lucy struggled into a sitting position as Amy-Beth drew the curtains, letting some sunlight into the bedroom.

"What? What time is it, Amy-Beth. Is there a fire or something, what's the panic?"

Amy-Beth thrust the doll in front of her sister. "There," she said, almost triumphantly, "what do you make of that?"

"It's a doll," mumbled Lucy, pulling the bedclothes around her shoulders against the chill of the morning air. Then, sitting bolt upright, "but not just any doll" she said as, sleep wearing off, she recognised the familiar little dress, hair colour and shiny little face of the doll in the mirror. "Where on earth did you get her?" she asked Amy-Beth, panic starting to set in.

"Sophie's bedroom" her sister replied.

"What - *Sophie's* bedroom? But who put it there - are we even sure it's the same one? It can't be, I mean things in mirrors don't come to life, I mean they can't come out of mirrors and walk . . ."

"Lucy, *reflections* are what you're supposed to see in mirrors, not horror stories. Look, I'm trying to be rational about this, too, but it's rather difficult when you just can't understand anything. Maybe we should tell Aunt Patsy now – do you think she'll believe?

"Oh I don't know. I'm afraid to even touch the doll – what are we going to do with her – I don't think we should leave her in Sophie's room, and quite honestly I don't fancy having her in here with me."

Amy-Beth sighed. "Suppose she'll have to stay in my room for now, then. If Sophie asks, though I don't think she will since she's totally besotted with Sweetie, we'll say we thought we'd make a new dress for her as this one's a bit shabby."

Lucy looked incredulous. "A new dress! When have you or I ever been any good at sewing, or the least bit interested in making new clothes for dolls? I think you'll have to come up with something better than that, she'll never fall for that one in a month of Sundays!"

Amy-Beth was forced to smile. "Yes, I suppose you're right, it is a bit far-fetched, though, God knows, so much has been happening recently it's no wonder I'm losing touch with reality. Okay, I'll go put the doll in my room and we'll go downstairs for breakfast. We'll wait till Sophie asks before we go into any explanations of the doll's whereabouts – should she even miss her – and next time she takes Sweetie out for a walk we'll have a quiet word with Aunt Patsy about all the strange goings on."

And so they did. Sophie had barely finished eating her pancakes and syrup (a firm favourite with Aunt Patsy), than she was gone, Sweetie scampering behind her, tail wagging in anticipation of the fun he knew they would both have outside.

"Aunt Patsy" began Amy-Beth. "How's your imagination these days?"

Chapter 5

Aunt Patsy wiped some syrup from the corner of her mouth and looked at her nieces expectantly. "Imagination? What a funny thing to ask. But then, you young ones think you get past the age of fourteen and you lose your imagination. Well let me tell you, mine is just as good now as it ever was. So go on, elaborate please." Leaning both her elbows on the breakfast table, looking from one girl to the other, she waited for one of them to speak.

Ten minutes later, and with parts of the story being told by both sisters at the same time, so that very little was understood, Aunt Patsy's elbows remained on the table. "Well, girlies, that certainly is a story for someone with a vivid imagination," she said finally. "I don't even think you could have made that one up."

"You mean you believe us?" asked Lucy. "We're not sure if we can believe it ourselves, and we really don't want to scare Sophie any more than she already is, but we just don't know what to do."

Just at that, the kitchen door burst open and

Sophie almost fell inside. "Sweetie, I've lost Sweetie, I let her off her lead for a minute so we could run about more and next thing I knew she was off. I think she must have been chasing something, a rabbit or some such, and I called and called but she didn't come back and, oh, Aunt Patsy, please help, I just have to find her." The young girl collapsed, sobbing into Aunt Patsy's arms.

"Now then, calm down, pet, we'll find her. Just wait two ticks while I get my jacket and I'll be right with you. And if we don't get her this morning, she'll be back for lunch she'll be hungry, you'll see, she won't stay away long." Aunt Patsy reached inside the cupboard and took her thick jacket from the hook. "You two girls better stay inside. It's cold outside, and anyway your mother might 'phone." Pushing Sophie in front of her, Aunt Patsy turned back to Amy-Beth. "Don't mention any of this to your Mum. If she does telephone, there'll be time enough for her to know everything when she gets back."

Chapter 5

Lucy and Amy-Beth began to clear away the breakfast dishes.

"Amy-Beth", began Lucy, "where did you put the music box last night when we left the study?"

"I don't think I picked it up, to tell you the truth, and if I did, I certainly don't know where I put it. Let's finish clearing this mess away for now and then we'll go have a look. Maybe by that time they'll be back with Sweetie."

From outside the window, the two girls could hear alternate voices calling the little puppy's name. First Aunt Patsy, loud and shrill, then little Sophie, sometimes sounding as though she were trying to choke back her tears.

Mum did 'phone later in the morning, to say they were having such a good time they had decided to stay for the rest of the week-end, provided it suited Aunt Patsy to stay with the children. Amy-Beth explained about the missing puppy, and that Aunt Patsy was outside searching for it, but really no-one thought there would be a problem with Mum and Dad staying a bit longer. Mum rang off, saying she would 'phone and speak with Aunt Patsy later that day.

By lunchtime, the pup still hadn't been found. Aunt Patsy had forced Sophie to return to the house, after both had searched the large grounds a number of times, and made the young girl drink some warm soup.

"She'll turn up, Sophie, I know she will, just you wait and see." Sophie, however, was beyond consoling, and finding it very hard to stop herself from crying.

Amy-Beth and Lucy tried to console her as best they could.

"Aunt Patsy's right," said Amy-Beth. "She will turn up. Dogs don't like to be outside in the cold, she'll be back before tea-time, you'll see."

Lucy put an arm around her young sister's shoulders. "Let's go play something else until Sweetie comes back – your music box – let's go find that and watch the ballerina twirl you've always smiled at that before."

Sophie tried to dry her eyes on her already sodden hankie. "Okay," she answered reluctantly, "but I don't know where that is either – you'll have to help me look."

Aunt Patsy smiled gratefully at Lucy. "Go on then, girls, go and look for the ballerina. I'll keep watch through the kitchen window in case Sweetie does reappear for her lunch. And remember, you've got me for the rest of the weekend, so start thinking of what we can do, maybe I can curl your hair for you, Sophie, what do you think?"

Chapter 6

"The music box is in the study, I think," said Amy-Beth. And, as the words left her mouth, she suddenly knew where they would find Sweetie. "Lucy, why don't you take Sophie upstairs to the bedroom just now, and I'll bring up the ballerina."

"But. . ." Lucy started to protest, then, seeing the look of warning on Amy-Beth's face, decided to say no more and take the young girl upstairs.

Amy-Beth pushed open the study door gingerly, afraid of what she might see. Nothing! The room was quiet, the mirror calm, and the music box was on the table where she had left it. She picked up the little box and looked at it carefully. "I wonder," she thought, then decided to go with her instincts and wind up the music box.

As the tune started to play, she replaced the box on the table and turned to look at the mirror.

Once again, a mist appeared to coat the exterior of the mirror - clearing to reveal the little girl who had appeared before. On the girl's knee Amy-Beth saw what she had known she would - the little girl had Sweetie!

"But you can't have her," Amy-Beth started, not even sure if the girl could hear her or not, but unable to control herself. "She's my little sister's puppy – she's distraught at having lost her – you'll have to give her back."

The girl in the mirror slowly raised her eyes to meet Amy-Beth's.

"And just why should I give her back? She has my doll!"

Amy-Beth stepped back in amazement. So the girl could see her, too, and communicate!

"She didn't steal your doll," said Amy-Beth angrily. "Someone put it in her room – how could she steal something that lives in a mirror anyway – it doesn't make any sense."

"And just what does make sense to you, Amy-Beth, I mean you are speaking to a mirror, aren't you?"

"How do you know my name? Who are you? What's going on? Why are you doing this to my family?"

The girl smiled again. "Oh dear, we are upset, aren't we? If you'll take time to listen, I'll answer you as best I can. I know your name because you've been in here so many times before and your sisters *do* call you by name, you know. To answer your second question, my name is Sara and you've already guessed who I really am – the Keeper of the Mirror – or the Keeper of Lost Souls, anyway, being one myself. I'm not doing anything to your family. You girls started this off by playing the music box. It's always been the same throughout the centuries – if someone plays that tune it starts the mirror off, showing all the awful deaths it has witnessed over the years. How many have you seen so far – two? That means you've got about another 2,375 to go! Oh dear, you will be frightened by the end of it all, won't you?"

Amy-Beth was struggling to keep her composure, but she knew if she wanted to get the puppy back and return the family to some semblance of normality she must get as much information from the girl as possible.

"You say Lost Souls – what do you mean?" she managed to ask.

The girl looked up from stroking the dog's head. "Oh, you know, souls which have never found complete rest because of the way they died, people who have had violent and unnecessary deaths, and whose families sometimes carry a burden of guilt, that sort of thing. I myself was brought up in this house back in the 1800s. My mother was the housekeeper, though she was treated, as was I, more like one of the family. We were happy here, you know, the two of us. My father had died of tuberculosis the year after I was born so my mother was extremely lucky to find this position, and with such a nice family. Anyway, it all went really well until she got involved with the new gardener. I had never liked the man, but I suppose mother was feeling a bit lonely, so she took to going for walks with him, and sometimes spent time with him on her day off. He knew I didn't like him – the feeling was mutual actually – and sometimes he would tell mother lies about my behaviour to make her cross.

"It all came to an end the day. I walked into the kitchen to find him shaking my mother violently, shouting at her that she would have to 'make her choice'. Of course, I had no idea what the argument was about, I just knew that I had to make this evil man stop hurting my mother. I shouted to him to leave her alone, but he ignored me so I ran at him and pounded his back with my fists. He was such a big man, though, that my punches had no effect and he continued to shake my mother, getting more and more angry all the time. And so I went to the kitchen table, and picked up the biggest knife I could find. I ran at him, then, shouting all the time to leave my mother alone but, when I lunged at him, he jumped out of the way so quickly that the knife plunged not into him but into my mother.

" 'You've killed your mother, you've killed Hannah,' he shouted at me – I can still hear his voice to this day – and I drew back in horror, still holding the blood spattered knife. Mother was lying on the stone floor of the kitchen, blood flowing from her wound. 'She's dead', he kept shouting, 'you've killed your own mother' so I picked up the knife again and drove it deep into my heart, as far as it would go."

Amy-Beth gasped and stepped towards the girl. "But Sara, it was an accident, you didn't mean to kill her. And was that how you died then – you killed yourself?"

"Yes," replied Sara, "and the tune played

by the music box was one of mother's favourites and was playing in the kitchen that day. The mirror you see in front of you, which dates way back before even my time judging from the scenes I've witnessed it replaying, was hanging in the large hall just outside the kitchen. For some reason, it took my tortured soul into it, and I am forced to witness the same horrific scenes it replays over and over again every time someone plays that tune. There can never be any rest for me, never, and I don't deserve it anyway."

Sara looked so sad, Amy-Beth almost pitied her. "There must be something we can do to help you," she said gently. "You can't spend the rest of eternity like this, reliving horror every day of your existence. There must be something, Sara, only I don't know what." As Amy-Beth finished speaking, Sara's face started to fade, the mist returned once more before finally disappearing and leaving the mirror as normal.

"I'll be back, Sara, don't give up hope!"

Amy-Beth was saying, hoping the young girl could still hear her. And she would, she vowed to herself, she didn't know what could be done to help, but she wouldn't give up till she'd thought of something.

Chapter 7

The three sisters spent the afternoon upstairs entertaining one another. Lucy had brought out one of their favourite books from when they were really small and they had read it between them, each taking on a different character. Aunt Patsy, as promised, curled Sophie's hair and Amy-Beth and Lucy painted all Sophie's fingernails different colours, anything in an attempt to keep her mind off her missing puppy.

Just before tea-time, there was a knock on the door, and Aunt Patsy answered. Sophie turned expectantly, hoping for news of Sweetie. A young man, tall and imposing, stood in the doorway. Aunt Patsy smiled, "yes, can I help you?"

"Are you Mrs Johnson?" the man asked, smiling back.

"No, I'm Mrs Johnson's sister, what can I do for you?"

"Oh, I see, well you won't know me, but Mr Johnson asked me to come up and have a look around sometime this weekend. I'm the new gardener, you see."

"Oh, come in, come in," said Aunt Patsy. "No, Harry didn't mention it to me, though he *was* supposed to be here himself this weekend so perhaps that's why. No matter, anyway, we're here, and you can have a look round no problem. Now, would you like some tea, I'm sure one of the girls. . ."

Aunt Patsy looked to where Amy-Beth had just sat down at the kitchen table. The girl's eyes were wide as saucers, she was positively *staring* at the new arrival, and she had completely lost all colour from her cheeks.

"What on earth is wrong with you, Amy-

Beth?" she asked. "You've gone deathly white, you look as though you've seen a ghost or something!"

Amy-Beth managed to tear her eyes away from the man. "What did you say, Aunt Patsy, sorry I was miles away, thinking about something else just now."

"I was offering our visitor something warm to drink, that's all, there's a chill in the air today, and I thought one of you girls would be good enough to put the kettle on!"

Lucy, realising something was wrong with her sister, obliged Aunt Patsy by getting up and filling the kettle for her. She must get Amy-Beth out of here and find out what was wrong.

Amy-Beth meanwhile was trying to compose herself. "A new *gardener*" she kept saying to herself. Dad had never mentioned getting a gardener. I mean, she knew the grounds were huge and everything, but she didn't know he had been thinking about employing someone.

She was grateful when Lucy asked if she would give her some help with a passage she had been struggling with in her new book for, though she knew Lucy never needed help with anything to do with the English language, the excuse allowed her to escape from the kitchen.

The two girls went into the study, for they knew it was the one place Sophie would not follow them.

"Okay – spill the beans," began Lucy. "You turned a ghastly colour in there – gave me quite a fright when I looked at you."

Amy-Beth covered her face with her hands. "Oh, I don't know any more Lucy, I just don't know. I don't know if my imagination is running away with me, if I'm completely losing my sanity, or what."

"So tell me then and maybe I can help," replied her sister.

Amy-Beth recounted all that happened, telling Lucy how it was a gardener's fault that young Sara had killed her mother, and subsequently herself, and how it was Sara who had Sophie's puppy all the time.

"Gosh, no wonder you changed colour when a gardener walked into the kitchen – I mean, I didn't find it that strange at all, but you're obviously concerned because of what Sara told you. Tell you what, though, Amy-Beth, if I hadn't witnessed that last sighting with you, I'd be incredibly sceptical about all this."

"Yes, I know, sometimes I can't believe what I'm saying. It just doesn't seem real. But the fact is that this *is* happening. Sara does have the puppy and we have a strange gardener in our kitchen. What are we going to do? I've promised to help Sara in any way I can, and I need you to help me figure out what we're going to do next. Let's get back to the kitchen and see what's happening. I feel calmer now I've spoken to you."

The girls returned then to the kitchen, only to find it empty. They grabbed their jackets and went outside to look for Aunt Patsy. They found her, with Sophie and the new gardener, looking over one particular area of the garden that was very badly overgrown.

"It's a long time since this has been touched," the man was saying. "Everything's completely overgrown, I'll need to put a lot of work into this, that is, if Mr Johnson chooses to employ me."

Aunt Patsy smiled and pushed her hair behind her ear. "Oh, I'm sure you'll get the job, Jim. Tell you what, why don't you make a start on this particular area since you're here – that'd be sure to impress Harry when he got back. It's a real eyesore!"

"*Jim*" Amy-Beth cringed. "So they are on first name terms already" she thought. And asking him to make a start 'since you're here'! Aunt Patsy didn't know what she was doing – this man could be dangerous – but how on earth could Amy-Beth tell her the remainder of the seemingly ridiculous mirror story – she hadn't exactly been impressed by the first part the girls had told her. She decided to keep her mouth shut for the time being, after all Mum and Dad would be home tomorrow and she and Lucy would simply have to tell them everything, ridiculous sounding or not!

"That's a great idea, Patsy, you show me where all the garden tools are, and I'll make a start on clearing this ground, may as well make the most of the dry weather while it lasts."

Aunt Patsy, Sophie and Jim all walked off in the direction of one of the old stone buildings which Dad had used to store all his garden tools and DIY implements.

"Well," said Lucy, "what do you make of that?."

Amy-Beth shrugged. "Nothing we can do, I suppose, till Mum and Dad get back tomorrow night. Maybe there's nothing suspicious here, anyway, I mean if Sara had mentioned 'milkman' would we be behaving like this, refusing to drink hot chocolate in case it was spiked with anything? I don't think so! We're probably over-reacting to the whole situation.

Come on, let's go for a walk, I feel I've been cooped up in the house long enough."

They shouted to Aunt Patsy where they were going. She raised a gloved hand to wave before entering the stone building to fetch the tools.

Amy-Beth and Lucy walked further than they had intended, so occupied were they with their own thoughts. Before they realised, they had reached the outskirts of the nearest village and, before turning back, went into the small village shop and bought some crisps, magazines and toffee. "The toffee will sustain us on our way home," they laughed together and started to make their way back home.

As they rounded the corner to begin the long walk up the driveway, they saw that Jim was still working in the garden. He had taken off his jacket and, sleeves rolled up, was making short work of pulling out all the dead shrubbery, clearing away all the leaves and putting all the rubbish into large bags Aunt Patsy must have given him.

"Hi there, girls" he smiled as he sighted the two sisters. They smiled back, feeling ridiculous for thinking so badly of him earlier that day.

"Hi" said Lucy, walking towards where he worked. "You're making a great job there" she said. "Don't think this part of the garden has been touched for years and years."

Jim stopped and leant on his spade, wiping the sweat from his forehead. "You're right there – Lucy is it?" She nodded. "I'll start to dig soon – try and get the earth turned over before it gets dark. No point in wasting good sunlight, is there?"

"Would you like a toffee?" asked Amy-Beth, trying to make up for being so rude earlier.

"Thanks, but no. A cool drink would be nice, though, if you wouldn't mind."

"Of course we wouldn't mind" replied Amy-Beth. "I'll be back in a minute – are you staying there, Lucy."

Lucy nodded, unable to speak because of

the large quantity of toffee she had just put in her mouth. "Bring me some too," she barely managed to say. Amy-Beth laughed at her sister's bulging jaws and gave her the 'thumbs up' sign as she turned towards the house.

She filled a large pitcher with some cold juice from the fridge and placed it on a tray with some glasses before returning outside. Jim was explaining to Lucy what some of the things were that he had pulled from the garden, and trying to make her understand how he knew the difference between weeds and plants. Amy-Beth sat down on a small garden bench and invited the two to have a drink. Jim drank thirstily from his glass, then said he'd have to get back to work, though the two girls were welcome to stay and watch if they really wanted to.

Amy-Beth and Lucy settled onto the bench, enjoying the late afternoon sunshine, listening to the thud of the spade as Jim drove it down into the ground, turning the soil.

"Don't know what I've hit here – solid rock

Chapter 7

I think – can't get the spade to go down any further," he complained.

He pushed the spade back into the ground and put all his weight on top of it, but to no avail. The girls could hear the sound of the metal spade hitting rock, too, and got up to see what Jim would do as he bent down closer to the ground. He started to scrape away all the dirt and soil he could, trying to clear the area so that he could maybe try to prise the large rock out. The area the rock covered, however, was larger than he had first thought and he had eventually to bend on his hands and knees the better to see what he was doing.

"Good Lord – what's this?" the girls heard him say.

"What's wrong?" asked Lucy, trying to push nearer to see what was happening. Amy-Beth joined her sister on the ground beside Jim.

"What is it?" she too wanted to know.

The new gardener stood up. "I don't know if you girls should see this – maybe we should go get your aunt Patsy first. . ."

Amy-Beth knelt down and looked where Jim had been scraping away the dirt. There, lying flat, and covered in moss and slime, was a gravestone!

Chapter 8

"A gravestone, Lucy, look, he's uncovered a gravestone! Whose name's on it, let me see!" Amy-Beth was excited at the find – she had been desperate from the first to find out the history of the house, and now they had made such an unexpected discovery, it was sure to tell them something they didn't know.

"Give me over that juice pitcher," she instructed her sister, and began to pour the contents over the top of the stone, wiping away the dirt and as much moss as she could.

"Hannah Fotheringham," she read aloud as she uncovered the name at the top of the stone. Then, brushing away the dirt from further down the stone, she was able to read "Sara Fotheringham, beloved child of Hannah", followed by some dates she couldn't quite make out.

"Hannah? Sara? The girl in the mirror!" she said excitedly to Lucy. "We've found the grave of the girl in the mirror, *and* her mother" she cried as Lucy knelt beside her, she too scanning the stone in disbelief.

Jim scratched his head. "The girl in the mirror?" he said to both girls. "What on earth are you talking about?"

With a jolt, Amy-Beth looked up at Jim. Realising she should say nothing which would prevent her and Lucy from being able to look at the stone (and Aunt Patsy would be sure to stop them anyway!) she stood up and tried to look calm and unflustered.

"Oh, it's just a game we play sometimes, we dress up and look at ourselves in the mirror, pretending to be people who may have lived in the house hundreds of years ago.

Hannah and Sara just happen to be some of the characters we play, that's all. Isn't it strange that we should find a gravestone bearing their names!"

"Yes, I suppose it is," replied Jim, totally unconvinced. "Look, don't you two do any more, I'll go get your Aunt Patsy before we cover the stone up again. Then we can wait and see what your father wants done – don't even know if this is a proper graveyard or not, do we?"

As he walked off towards the house, Amy-Beth reached for the small garden fork Jim had brought with him to use on the garden. She began scraping the remainder of the moss from the stone, trying frantically to uncover more of the wording on the stone.

"Hannah Fotheringham" she read again. "Born 1801, died 1851. Then, look, further down, Sara Fotheringham, beloved child of Hannah, born 1820, died 1829."

"Don't you see what that means," she turned to Lucy excitedly. Sara couldn't have killed her mother – her mother didn't die until 22 years later.

"Sara killed herself for nothing – we've got to let her know – she should be able to put her soul to rest now – she didn't kill her mother after all. Come on."

Lucy stood up and brushed the dirt from her clothes. "We've got to get the music box and get into the study – we need to contact Sara and let her know what we've found."

As the two young girls made their way back into the house they were met by Aunt Patsy, Jim and young Sophie. Sophie still looked drawn and tearful from the loss of her puppy. Amy-Beth bent to cuddle her.

"We're going to find Sweetie, don't you worry, pet, we'll find her." Sophie looked hopeful for a minute.

"But where are you going to look for her? We've looked all over." Her face clouded again. "Aunt Patsy said she'd be back by lunch-time, then by tea-time, and she hasn't been seen anywhere."

Chapter 8

Amy-Beth gave her a reassuring hug. "We'll get her back for you sweetheart, I promise."

The two girls continued up the path. Aunt Patsy called after them, "aren't you coming with us, girls? Jim just told me what you found out there."

"Em, yes, we'll be back in a second, Aunt Patsy, there's something we have to do in the house first," replied Lucy.

The girls quickly made their way to the study, throwing the door open wide on their arrival.

"Where's the ballerina, Amy-Beth?" asked Lucy.

"It should be over there on the table where I left it – ah, there it is. Give it to me, Lucy, we have to wind it up quickly. We have to reach Sara."

Once wound, the music box started to play, and the girls replaced it on the desk. They looked at the mirror anxiously.

"Please appear, please appear Sara, we really have to talk to you this time. Please!"

And, as the girls waited, they saw the mist that they had found so frightening before, appear suddenly before them, swirling in front of the mirror, then clearing to reveal Sara's young face.

"Amy-Beth! Look! She has Sweetie with her." Lucy pointed at the mirror.

"Yes, I know, I know that, Lucy. Listen, that's not important just now. Sara, can you hear us?

Sara looked blankly back at the sisters. "Yes, I can hear you. What is it you want what's so urgent?"

"Sara," began Amy-Beth. "You have to listen to me very carefully. I'll try to speak as slowly and as clearly as I can. A few moments ago we were outside in the part of the garden that lies just in front of the house, you know, under the old oak tree. Do you know where I mean, Sara?"

The girl nodded.

"We have a new gardener, you see, and today he was starting to clear that area. It was almost completely overgrown and he was pulling out all the dead bushes and plants for my Dad. The ground looks like it hasn't been touched for years. Anyway, you'll never guess what he found – a gravestone, Sara, a gravestone bearing your own and your mother's names."

Sara didn't flinch. "So? Why are you bothering to tell me this? I know I'm dead, and I know my mother's dead – I killed her, remember?"

Yes, but that's just the point. Listen to me, Sara. You didn't kill her, you didn't kill your mother. You couldn't have – she didn't die until 1851 and you died 22 years earlier in 1829! Don't you see, she didn't die that day in the kitchen – she was still alive!"

"But that's not possible!" the girl protested. "I was there, I drove the knife into her heart, I was the one who killed her, he said I'd done it. Why are you doing this to me, Amy-Beth, why can't you leave things alone?"

"Look Sara, maybe you just didn't hang

around long enough to see whether your mother was really dead. I think, Sara, that maybe you did hurt your mother, and maybe hurt her very badly, but she survived, Sara, she didn't die. Listen to me, I *saw* the dates on the gravestone. She didn't die!"

Sara shook her head and covered her ears with her hands, as though trying to shut out Amy-Beth's words. "This can't be true, it can't be."

Lucy, then, approached the mirror too. "Sara, I saw the stone too. You have to believe both of us – we're telling you the truth. What reason would we have to lie?"

"Oh I wish you could come outside with us and see the stone, Sara. Maybe that would be the only way you could believe us. But wait a minute. Has the mirror never replayed the scene where you supposedly kill your mother?"

"Yes, of course it has" replied Sara. "On and off over the years, the scene has unfolded before me, only when it gets to the point where I lift the kitchen knife I find myself starting to scream and scream.

I have to cover my eyes, so that I can neither see nor hear a thing. Don't you see, Amy-Beth, I have to shut it out. I try to shut out *his* voice, my mother crying. I can never come to terms with what happened – how would you feel, having to watch yourself *kill* your own mother, over and over again? It's awful, completely unbearable."

"I know," nodded Amy-Beth in agreement. "But what I'm trying to say is, maybe if you could force yourself, just once, to watch the scene right through, you would see that your mother didn't die. I mean, can you conjure it up – can we do this, can we make the mirror show us that particular scene?"

"I don't know." Sara shook her head. "I don't think this is a good idea, I really don't think I want to do this."

"I think Amy-Beth's right, Sara, it has to be worth a try," said Lucy. "I know it must be hard for you, but look at how many years you've spent, tortured, never getting any rest, and this could be your chance. We can help you – please let us try!"

"I have to go now," Sara looked sad and bewildered.

"Don't go, don't go, Sara!" pleaded Amy-Beth. "Stay, please, stay, we have to talk about this."

"I don't want to talk about it any more" said Sara. "I have to go and think. I'll see you tomorrow, come and see me tomorrow. We'll talk about it again then."

As Sara's voice faded, so too did her reflection in the mirror. Amy-Beth and Lucy looked sadly at one another.

"Wasn't much more you could have said, Amy-Beth." said Lucy.

"I know, I know, I don't even know whether replaying the scene will show what we think it will show, but we have to try our best to do something. Let's join the others in the garden, come on I need some fresh air."

Chapter 9

Jim, Aunt Patsy and Sophie were, all three, on their hands and knees in the middle of the small garden. The amount of dead shrubbery Jim had cleared had made a huge difference and, by the time dusk fell that night, the little party had in fact uncovered another three gravestones. A Mr and Mrs Deloitte were buried there, as was their son, Edward.

"I suppose they must have been the family that lived here, and the Fotheringhams were their employees," said Amy-Beth.

Aunt Patsy glanced at her niece. "How did you know that? How do you know it wasn't the other way about?"

"Oh, eh, just a guess," she said. "Maybe you're right, maybe the Deloittes were the servants, I've no idea. Anyway, let's go in for supper, I'm starved."

Aunt Patsy stood up and brushed the dirt from her trousers. "I'm hungry too, I know, I've got an idea, girls, why don't we get a takeaway? Fancy a pizza, anybody? What about you, Jim, would you like to stay with us for supper?"

Jim looked at Aunt Patsy, then at the faces of the three young girls looking expectantly back at him. "What do you think, girls?"

Amy-Beth and Lucy had by now decided that he was actually all right, their new gardener, so they agreed with Aunt Patsy that it would be nice to have an extra guest for supper. The four sat round the table in their warm kitchen eating large slices of pizza, consuming enormous quantities of juice and discussing the day's events.

"I think we should get up bright and early tomorrow and clear away the rest of the rubbish" said Aunt Patsy. "It's not fair that people are laid to rest and then everything's left to get so overgrown. Maybe we could plant some new flowers, make the garden look really nice again."

"What a good idea," said Lucy. "Wonder why the last owners let it get into such a mess anyway."

"Well, the last owners probably didn't know it was a graveyard. I think it goes back a lot further than that, judging by the state we found it in. Anyway, we'll give it our best shot tomorrow, won't we, get it looking nice and tidy for your Mum and Dad getting back."

Next day at breakfast Sophie was morose.

"What's wrong, pet?" asked Aunt Patsy.

"It's Sweetie." She shook her head dismally. "I just thought she would have come back by now. Maybe she didn't like me, maybe it's my fault."

"Don't be silly," reassured Aunt Patsy. "Of course she liked you, how could anyone not like you – she'll come home, I promise you she will, she'll come home." Though by now, even Aunt Patsy was starting to question whether or not the little pup would ever come back.

Once the girls had finished breakfast they all went outside again to start washing down the gravestones, clearing off the moss. Jim was arriving later that morning. He promised to come and help them finish turning over the soil so that everything would be ready for planting and the graves would look as though they were looked after, just as they should have been.

Round about eleven o'clock, Amy-Beth and Lucy told Aunt Patsy they were going inside to make some hot drinks and would be back out shortly. In reality, the girls were going into the study to try and speak once again with Sara. They entered the study and wound up the music box quickly, staring once again at the mirror.

"Sara, please come, it's us, we're back, we

promised we'd come back this morning and we're here."

First of all, the mist, and then Sara appeared in the mirror.

"Good morning," she said to the two sisters.

"Good morning," they replied. "How are you today?" asked Amy-Beth.

"How do you think I am? Mixed up, confused, frightened."

"I know," said Amy-Beth. "You must be all of those things, but please, please, I really think this is your only chance. Can't you try and get the mirror to show the scene? Will you try, please?"

"Well, I've thought long and hard, and I've decided that, yes, you're probably right, I really do have to do this. So here goes."

Sara sat down and, placing her hands calmly before her she closed her eyes and bowed her head in deep concentration. She thought of her mother, she thought of the awful gardener, she thought of nice Mrs

Deloitte and her husband, and she thought of Edward, who used to play with her and let her ride his horse. She thought very, very hard of all the things she had purposely blocked from her mind for all those hundreds of years.

"Please," she whispered. "Please, please, let me see what happened that day, please."

And all of a sudden there she was! On the other side of the mirror, the same little girl stood, clutching a posy of summer flowers. She was outside the house, enjoying what looked to be a beautiful sunny day and, though she had spent most of her morning in the kitchen helping her mother, she was now determined to enjoy the sunshine. She had picked the flowers for her Mum and was about to take them to her in the kitchen.

Heading towards the kitchen, Sara stopped in the hall, for she could hear raised voices coming from where she knew her mother to be. She started to walk more quickly, alarmed in case her mother was in any sort of danger or trouble. As she drew nearer, she realised it was *his* voice, the gardener, the one she had never liked, the one who insisted on taking her mother out walking, and the one who had told her mother what a badly behaved, spoilt little girl she was. She wasn't bad or spoilt at all – she adored her mother – she just knew that this man was bad, evil, and she didn't want him anywhere near her. His voice was getting louder, what was he saying? She could just about make him out.

"You have to make your choice, Hannah," she heard him shout. "You have to pick – it's either her or me. She's so spoilt – why can't you see it? You couldn't possibly ask me to tolerate that child. Anyway, my wages aren't enough to pay for three of us to live the way you've been accustomed."

Sara froze – he was trying to take her mother away from her – trying to split them up. No! No! Her voice screamed inside her head – she had to get to her mother and tell her not to listen!

Her mother's voice was next to be heard,

angry, too. "Look, Dick, I've told you a hundred times, it's over. I want no more to do with you. I've chosen Sara over you there never was a choice, let's face it. I never loved you, I hate you, I want you out of my life and out of my daughter's life. Please, leave me alone, or you'll force me into telling Mrs Deloitte how you hound me."

"Oh, that's the way of it, is it?" shouted Dick at the top of his voice. "Won't give you a minute's peace? That's rich – it's you who's been after me. Obvious to everyone it is! What about the day you asked me for a ride into the village for provisions, eh? What about that, then?"

"Dick, I needed provisions, and I couldn't carry them on my own. If I'd thought you would have read so much into it, I wouldn't have asked, believe me. As it is, you've never let me forget it! I will never ask you another favour so long as I live. Now please, just get out of my kitchen and let me get on with my job."

"But it's not your kitchen, is it? It's hers, its Mrs Snooty's upstairs."

"Dick, please don't talk about Mrs Deloitte like that. She's been so good to us."

"Huh, she may have been good to you, and that brat of yours, but she couldn't care tuppence for the likes of me."

Then, his voice softening, he began to beg. "Hannah, please, please change your mind. I can't bear to live without you. I love you, I adore you, please marry me, come away with me, we'll be so happy together."

By this time Sara had pushed open the door just enough to make out her mother and Dick standing at the the end of the kitchen – he tightly holding onto her mother's arms and shaking her from time to time, as though to make her see what he thought was sense.

"Let go of me, Dick. Let go of my arms, now. You're hurting me – can't you see you're hurting me!"

It was at that point that Sara burst into the room, screaming and flailing her fists. "Leave my mother, leave her alone, you're hurting her – didn't you hear what she said?"

"Yes, I am hurting her, aren't I, because she hurt me, and I'll hurt her even more if she doesn't do what I say. So leave us alone, brat, this has nothing to do with you. I'll sort this."

Sara flew at him then. "I won't tell you again, leave my mother alone." She began pummelling the man's back with her small fists as hard as she could, harder and harder. But she was slight and he was such a big man that her punches had no effect on him whatsoever and he merely continued to hold Hannah, her hands pinned behind her back.

"Tell the brat to leave us, tell her to get out of the kitchen before I do something we'll all regret!"

Hannah, unable to free her wrists from his grasp, instead pulled back her leg and delivered as hard a kick as she could to Dick's shins.

"Ow," he yelled and, angrier than ever, he let go of the woman's wrists and slapped her hard across her face. When Hannah lifted her head up from the blow, Sara could see a trickle of blood coming from the side of her mother's mouth. This was more than she could bear.

She started to hit him, and kick him, and punch him, screaming all the time at him to leave her mother alone. Her mother tried to reassure her she was all right but, by this time, Sara was in a complete frenzy and had dashed to the kitchen table looking for something with which to strike this monster who was doing these terrible things to her mother. The first thing which came to hand was, of course, a knife, the largest knife there was in the kitchen.

She ran at Dick, almost blind with panic and fear and, just as she got within striking distance, he seemed to sense both her and the danger behind him and jumped out of the way. The knife plunged straight into her mother.

Dick, almost triumphant, was shouting "You've killed her, look what you've done, I always knew you were bad, you've killed your own mother. I knew you were a bad lot, look what you've done, look at the blood pouring from her, how does it feel to be a murderer?"

Sara, almost numb with the shock of what had just happened, began to walk backwards, trying to get as far away from the body as she could, until she could go no further, feeling her back pressed firmly against the wall. Dick, sneering now, jibed again.

"You've killed her, are you happy now missy? You've killed the only person that ever loved you – and you were supposed to love her! Why did you do it?"

Sara could take no more and, still clutching the knife, she turned the handle away from her and plunged the blade straight into her own heart. She died instantly.

Just as the young girl fell to the floor, another two people joined them in the kitchen. Young Mr Edward and his stablehand stood in the doorway, having heard the commotion from outside.

Chapter 9

Edward ran to where young Sara lay and picked up her limp body. He didn't seem to notice that his own clothes were becoming drenched in the girl's blood as he hugged her tightly to him.

"Sara, oh Sara, what's become of you?" he wept. He felt for a pulse in her neck but could find none. Reluctant to put her down, he cradled her against him for a while longer then gently carried her from the kitchen into the sitting room where he placed her gently on one of the sofas. Returning to the kitchen, and realising that Hannah was still alive, though her breathing was very shallow, he sent his young stablehand to fetch the doctor from the village.

The awful gardener was standing in the corner, looking almost pleased with himself! Hard to believe that he was supposed to love the lady lying on the stone flags before him.

"Get out," said Edward through clenched teeth. "Get out of here, and never let me set eyes on you again, if you know what's good for you."

Dick did leave, having witnessed Mr Edward's bad temper before, and deciding it was probably best to get out now before the Law got involved. He had a past he would prefer the police didn't know about!

Edward carried Hannah to his own mother's bedroom and waited there for the doctor to arrive. When he did arrive, a short while later, he had a quick look at Sara but only confirmed what Edward already knew. "Afraid she's dead, my lad, nothing we can do there."

Edward led the way to his mother's bedroom, and quickly wiped a tear away before the doctor could see it.

"I just don't understand what happened. She was such a beautiful, kind, sweet little thing. I don't know what went on in the kitchen before we got there." The pair continued on up the stairs and Edward led the way into the bedroom so that the doctor could attend to Hannah. Although she had lost a lot of blood, the doctor was able to help. The wound was mostly superficial and

Chapter 9

hadn't gone deep enough to do any real damage.

A week or so later, Hannah Fotheringham lay propped up in bed, Mrs Deloitte and Edward chatted to her as she tried to eat some breakfast. Though she had been hurt at the time, and on the verge of blacking out, she had seen what had happened, and knew that her daughter had drove the knife into her own flesh. Her eyes filled with tears.

"I can't believe Sara would have done such a thing because she'd hurt me, I can't believe she's taken her life. She was my life. I adored her completely. Whatever will I do without her?" And she buried her head in her hands and sobbed.

Mrs Deloitte placed a comforting arm around the weeping mother's shoulders.

"I know, my dear, and I know you'll never forget Sara, or indeed the awful way in which she died. We'll have her buried in the small family cemetery in the garden so that she's always close by. You can plant whatever flowers you like, we'll keep it looking pretty for you, and for Sara's memory – for she was such a beautiful child. I know it's little condolence, but at least you'll feel she's always nearby."

Chapter 10

Amy-Beth, coming slowly back to the present, realised her eyes were wet. She rubbed at them quickly before Sara could see and walked closer to the mirror. The scene had faded completely now and Sara still sat, huddled in the corner, the little puppy licking at her fingers almost as though it, too, sensed that something was wrong.

"Sara," Amy-Beth said gently, "are you all right?"

Sara lifted her eyes from her hands and turned to look at Amy-Beth. "I, I can't believe what I've just seen. She didn't die - I didn't kill my mother after all, and look what I've had to endure for all these years, and for nothing! Oh, I don't know how to feel relieved that I didn't kill her, sad at her losing me and having to spend the rest of her life without her only child, angry that I've had to spend so much time stuck inside this mirror, neither alive nor dead." She barely finished this last sentence before she burst into tears, great racking sobs which shook her whole body.

As before, Lucy, too, stepped towards the mirror, as though trying to reach out to the girl to comfort her in some way.

"Poor, poor Sara," she murmured. "You've been through such a lot."

Amy-Beth sat down in the large armchair opposite the mirror. She held the little music box in her hand, and played with it absentmindedly while she waited for Sara to calm herself. Eventually, she decided it was time to speak.

"Sara, I know you're desperately upset about all this, but you have to look at things positively. This means you're free – don't you see, you don't have to spend any more time stuck inside that, that timewarp – you can walk away now, today, to be with your Mum, to take your place beside her, where you should have been years ago."

Sara looked at both sisters and swallowed hard. "You're right, I know that, I just don't know if I have the courage, I've gotten so used to being here. And anyway, how do I escape from the mirror? I know my mind has been freed, since I now know the truth, but my soul is caught up in this awful web and I don't know how to untangle it!"

"I think I know how" said Amy-Beth looking first at Lucy then back at the mirror. "But I'm going to be in serious trouble with Mum and Dad for what I think I need to do. Heaven only knows if they'll ever believe a word of this story!"

Standing up and moving further back from the mirror, she clasped Lucy's hand, taking her backwards with her.

"Goodbye, Sara," she whispered, motioning Lucy to do the same, and both girls bade farewell to their friend.

Lifting the music box high in the air, Amy-Beth threw it with all her might right at the centre of the mirror. It hit it with such force that it had exactly the effect she had hoped for. It shattered into a million pieces, large shards of glass scattering in every direction in the study. Both girls covered their eyes and tried to shield themselves from the small, sharp pieces which now littered the room.

When they uncovered their eyes, there was nothing left of the mirror save for the gilt edging. Lucy heard a little bark and, bending down behind the desk, she found Sweetie!

"Oh, come on darling, are you all right? Oh, look, Amy-Beth, she's cut her paw on all this glass." Lucy took a hankie from her pocket and wrapped it tightly around the puppy's paw. "It's all right, it's not deep, I think she'll survive!"

"Well," sighed Amy-Beth, "do you think it worked – do you think we freed her?"

"I think so," replied Lucy, "I'm quite sure she's gone to her final resting place now, you've given her peace eventually."

"Not just me," said Amy-Beth. "You helped too, you know. Anyway, let's get outside and find Sophie. She's going to be one happy little girl when she sees who you've got with you."

As the girls emerged from the back entrance of the house, they saw Mum and Dad's car parked in the driveway, having returned from their week-end away. They were presently speaking to Aunt Patsy, Sophie and Jim, no doubt being shown around the newly cleared garden. Amy-Beth and Lucy walked towards them, watching as Sophie's eyes grew wide with excitement as she noticed Sweetie. She ran towards her little dog, almost knocking Dad out of the way in her hurry.

"Hi, Mum, Dad," said the two girls, "did you have a nice time?"

"Yes, sweetheart, we had a lovely time," replied her Mum, Dad smiling beside her.

As Sophie took her puppy from Lucy's arms, Mum noticed the bandaged paw. "Now what on earth happened to her?" she asked.

Amy-Beth and Lucy took an arm each, either side of their mother as they started to walk back to the house.

"Well, Mum," said Amy-Beth, "I'm afraid it's rather a long story. . ."